Florence the Friendship Fairy was originally published
as a Rainbow Magic special. This version has
been specially adapted for developing readers
in conjunction with a Reading Consultant.

Special thanks
to Rachel Elliot
and Fiona Munro

Reading Consultant: Prue Goodwin, lecturer in literacy and children's books.

ORCHARD BOOKS

This story first published in Great Britain in 2010 by Orchard Books
First published as an Early Reader in 2012
This edition published in 2019 by The Watts Publishing Group

3 5 7 9 10 8 6 4 2

© 2019 Rainbow Magic Limited.
© 2019 HIT Entertainment Limited.
Illustrations © Orchard Books 2012

HiT entertainment

A CIP catalogue record for this book is available from the British Library.

ISBN 978 1 40835 978 5

Printed in China

MIX
Paper from
responsible sources
FSC® C104740
www.fsc.org

The paper and board used in this book are made from wood from responsible sources

Orchard Books
An imprint of Hachette Children's Group
Part of The Watts Publishing Group Limited
Carmelite House, 50 Victoria Embankment, London EC4Y 0DZ

An Hachette UK Company
www.hachette.co.uk
www.hachettechildrens.co.uk

Florence
the Friendship Fairy

Daisy Meadows

ORCHARD

www.rainbowmagicbooks.co.uk

The
Fairyland
Palace

May po[le]

Band stand

Stalls

Treasure
hunt

Kirsty's House

Wetherbury Village

Story One

Magical Memories

Magical
Memories

Rachel Walker was staying
with her best friend Kirsty Tate.
One day they looked through
Kirsty's scrapbook, which was
full of lovely things.

Kirsty and Rachel had a special secret. They were friends with the fairies! The scrapbook reminded them of all the fun they had enjoyed together.

"I hope we'll have another fairy adventure soon," Kirsty whispered.

Then she frowned.

"There's an empty space here. I don't remember that," she said.

Worse still, when Rachel turned the next page she saw that one photo was damaged. Another one looked unfamiliar.

"I don't recognise her," said
Rachel. She pointed to a
picture of a pretty fairy.

Before either girl could say
another word, the fairy began
to sparkle. She flew straight out
from the page!

"I'm Florence the Friendship Fairy," she said. "My magical memory book protects people's special memories."

"How lovely," said Kirsty. "But I don't think the magic is working at the moment."

Rachel held up the damaged scrapbook, and Florence looked at it sadly.

"My memory book has been stolen by naughty goblins," she said. "So your scrapbook is no longer magically protected!"

"That's terrible!" said Kirsty.

"Goblins have come here and messed up your book," Florence said. "I must find them before they do more damage."

"We'll help!" Rachel promised.

Just then, Kirsty's mum came into the room and asked the girls to go to the village shop to buy some groceries. Florence had to hide in the scrapbook!

A few minutes later the girls headed into the village with Florence. Rachel soon spotted something on the ground.

"That's a picture from my scrapbook!" said Kirsty.

The girls were walking through the park when they heard the sound of squabbling.

They hid behind a bush and saw three goblins marching along, pushing each other as they went. One of them was carrying a smart-looking book.

"That's my magical memory book!" whispered Florence.

"Why don't *we* make a memory book?" said a small goblin. "It would be far better than this one. I've got lots of lovely dirt and weeds to put in it!"

"We should put in a photo of me ripping up this soppy fairy book!" another goblin sniggered.

"No!" cried Florence, flying out from behind the bush. "Don't do that!"

"Go away," one of the goblins snapped. "We're not letting a silly fairy interfere."

The goblins sprinted away, one of them still holding the magical memory book. As he ran, all Florence's treasures began to fall from the pages.

"They're ruining it!" she cried.

She swooped down and waved her wand to make all the items fairy-size and collect everything that had fallen out.

The girls followed the goblins as fast as they could.

The goblins kept banging
into each other, but didn't stop.

"How do we make them
drop the book?" asked Florence.
"I know," said Rachel.

Then she shouted at the goblins: "Look out! There are hundreds of fairies following right behind you!"

"They're going to cover you in beautiful pink sparkles and take a photo!" added Kirsty.

"Yuck! Run for it!" cried the goblins. They were too silly to turn around and see that there was only one fairy fluttering along beside Kirsty and Rachel.

But the goblin carrying the magical memory book didn't drop it, as the girls had hoped. Instead, he clutched it even more tightly.

The goblins ducked down a side street with Florence and the girls following closely behind them.

Kirsty grinned when she saw the road was a dead end!

Moments later, the goblins had their backs to the wall. The smallest one was still clutching the magical memory book.

"Why do you want my pink book, anyway?" Florence asked them. "Wouldn't you rather have a nice green one instead?"

"Of course we would," said another goblin. "But we haven't got a green book, so we're having yours!"

The goblin stuck out his tongue at the girls and Florence.

"If we could find you the perfect goblin memory book, with an icky green cover, would you do a swap?" Rachel asked.

The goblins looked thoughtful.

"I could make you one with prickly bits and slime patches," Florence said. "I could even use special magic so you could add your favourite smells. But only if you give me my book back."

"Oooh, could you make it smell like dirty feet?" one asked.

"Mouldy mushrooms, too!" said another.

"I want blocked drains!" cried the third.

Florence nodded.

"It's a deal," the goblins said. "Do it!"

Florence waved her wand and
an oozy green book appeared.
The fairy gave it to the
goblins in return for *her* book.

"Thanks, girls!" she said to Kirsty and Rachel. "I have to go now, but take a look in your shopping bag."

As Florence vanished, Kirsty reached inside her mum's bag.

She pulled out two invitations.
"Rachel!" she cried. "We're
invited to a Friendship Party
tomorrow at the Fairyland
Palace!"

Story Two
The
Friendship
Party

The Friendship Party

The next day was the grand
opening of a new village hall in
Wetherbury, the village where
Kirsty lived. The girls helped
Mrs Tate hang decorations.

Suddenly, Florence flew in through an open window. She looked pale and anxious.

"Some goblins have stolen my magical friendship ribbon!" she said. "Without it, our Fairy Friendship Party will be a flop. Will you help me?

We need to search Fairyland for the goblins."

"We'd love to," said Kirsty. "But we're helping my mum."

"I can cast a spell so that time stands still while you're away," said Florence.

"Brilliant!" Rachel replied.

With a shimmer of sparkles Florence transformed the girls into fairies, and whisked them away to Fairyland.

When Rachel and Kirsty reached Fairyland, they were pleased to see some old friends.

"Look, there's Phoebe the Fashion Fairy!" said Rachel.

The girls waved to Phoebe.

Their fairy friend was pushing a rail of party dresses. When she waved back to the girls, several dresses slipped off their hangers.

Then Zoe the Skating Fairy whizzed up and rollerskated right over the dresses! She dropped the box of china plates she was carrying.

CRASH!

"All the party preparations are going wrong because I've lost my magic ribbon!" wailed poor Florence.

"Where is the ribbon usually kept?" Kirsty asked.

"It's normally tied to the maypole," Florence explained.

The girls saw a golden pole and walked over to look at it.

"The goblins decided they wanted to play with the ribbon, and stole it," said Florence.

"We'll help find it," Rachel promised. "Those naughty goblins can't be far away!"

The three fairies fluttered into the air and began searching. A burning smell floated up to them from the Fairyland bakery. Things were going wrong everywhere they looked.

As the fairies were flying over some woods, they heard loud shouts and cheers. They swooped down and ducked behind a tree trunk.

There were the goblins!

They were using Florence's beautiful friendship ribbon for a tug-of-war game.

"Oh no, they'll rip it!" cried poor Florence.

Then the goblins dropped the ribbon and started squabbling over who had won the game.

"Never mind that," said the biggest goblin. "How about a game of blind man's buff? We can use the ribbon as a blindfold."

As the goblins began to play, one of them picked up a pile of acorns and threw them hard at his blindfolded friend.

"Ow!" wailed the goblin who had been hurt.

"Ha ha!" jeered another.

"I really need to get that ribbon," whispered Florence to the girls. "But how?"

Kirsty had an idea.

"I know just what to do!" she said.

"Florence, could you magic up two ordinary ribbons that look like your friendship ribbon?" Kirsty went on.

"Of course," said the fairy.

"We're going to suggest to the goblins that they have a three-legged race," Kirsty said. "They can use the ribbons to tie up their legs. Then we trip them up and grab the magical friendship ribbon back!"

Florence waved her wand until two matching ribbons appeared in a swirl of sparkles.

"Yoo hoo!" Rachel called to the goblins. "Why don't you have a three-legged race?"

The goblins thought a race would be exciting.

"We'll show you soppy fairies how to have fun!" one sneered.

The goblins tied their legs together and ran off. But Florence made acorns appear magically under their feet.

"Oooh! Owww!" the goblins wailed as they tripped and fell over.

"Quick!" Rachel cried. "Grab the ribbon!"

Florence zoomed through the air and quickly untied her magical friendship ribbon from the tangle of goblin legs.

"Got it!" she said. "Come on, let's fly back and tie it to the maypole!"

The goblins yelled and shook their fists at the fairies, but Florence, Kirsty and Rachel soared out of their reach.

The three of them flew all the way back to the maypole, where Florence proudly tied the ribbon back in its place.

"Hurrah!" cheered everyone.

"Is that Kirsty and Rachel I see?" came a booming voice from behind them.

The girls turned around to see King Oberon and Queen Titania coming across the grass towards the maypole.

Kirsty and Rachel smiled back politely at the royal fairies, and bobbed curtseys.

Florence explained how Kirsty and Rachel had helped her rescue the magical memory book and the magical friendship ribbon.

"All the fairies are grateful for your help," said Queen Titania, "We would be very honoured if you two could officially open our party."

Kirsty and Rachel joined hands and grinned.

"We declare the Fairy Friendship Party OPEN!" they said together.

Rachel and Kirsty had a wonderful time at the party until the king and queen told them it was time to go home.

"Goodbye for now, girls," said Florence. "Later on, I'll bring you a thank-you present!"

She waved her wand and a whirlwind of magical sparkles rose up. When they disappeared, the girls saw they were back in Wetherbury Friendship Hall, holding the banner they had been going to hang on the wall.

"Look!" Rachel said, pointing at the painted letters on the banner. Before they had been plain, but now they were decorated with sparkly glitter.

"Fairy magic," Kirsty whispered, and the girls shared a smile.

Friends Forever

"I'm really looking forward to this!" said Rachel. She and Kirsty were preparing for a party to celebrate the opening of Wetherbury's new hall.

To make things even more exciting, Florence the Friendship Fairy had promised to bring the girls a present. She wanted to thank them for rescuing her magical memory book and magical friendship ribbon from naughty goblins.

The girls walked in to find that the party had already begun. But something seemed to be wrong.

"Nobody seems to be enjoying themselves," said Kirsty. She looked around.

There were sour expressions on all the children's faces.

Suddenly the girls saw Florence flutter out from behind a plant.

"It's my fault everyone's miserable," said the fairy. "I made a special friendship bracelet for each of you, and I was going to give them to you today."

"How lovely!" said Rachel. "But how does that make it your fault that the party is going badly?"

"A goblin stole the bracelets," explained Florence, sadly.

"A friendship bracelet should only be worn by the person it was made for," the fairy explained. "Otherwise the magic goes wrong, and people nearby start arguing."

"Do you think the goblin who stole our bracelets is here at the party?" cried Rachel.

"He must be," said Florence.

The friends looked around the hall. A magician was just getting ready to perform and the grumpy children were sitting down to watch.

"There's the goblin!" Kirsty said, pointing.

A goblin with a pointy nose was sitting in the front row, dressed as a wizard. He was wearing a colourful bracelet!

The magician put on a good show, but nobody looked impressed. Before long he hurried off stage. The sulky children wandered away, too. Only the goblin stayed behind.

"I want to see some proper magic!" he grumbled.

"We could use proper magic to trick him," suggested Kirsty. "Florence, can you magic us up magicians' costumes, please?'

The goblin looked surprised when the girls walked over to him in magical-looking robes.

"Abracadabra!" said Kirsty,
and a dove flew out of her hat!

"Wow!" said the goblin.

He didn't know Florence was
hidden under Rachel's hair,
doing all the magic for Kirsty.

"If you want to see a really good trick, watch my wand carefully," Kirsty said.

The goblin stared eagerly at the wand. Suddenly, a string of silk handkerchiefs shot out of its tip and swirled around him!

The handkerchiefs tightened so the goblin couldn't move.

"What's happening?" he cried, trying to raise his arms.

"We're taking Florence's bracelet back!" replied Kirsty. She untied it from his wrist.

Two other goblins hurried into the room. When they saw the tied-up goblin, they released him at once.

"You'll never find the other bracelet!" one of them sneered. "I hid it in this fantastic chest I found, in . . ."

"Ssh, don't tell them where it is!" snapped the first goblin.

"What chest?" said Florence. "Where is it?"

The goblins said nothing.

Kirsty, Rachel and Florence went outside to search.

Kirsty's mum was outside, talking to the other children. They all looked happier now that the magic of the first friendship bracelet was working.

"We're having a treasure hunt," said Mrs Tate. "Follow the clues to find the chest!"

"We have to find that chest first!" said Rachel to Kirsty. "Florence, can you turn us into fairies so we can fly?"

"The first clue is 'chair'," said Mrs Tate, as Florence waved her wand and the girls shrank.

The treasure hunt clues were hidden around the garden and the hall. Each time you found one, it told you where to look for the next.

The girls took care not to be spotted by the other children. They fluttered under all the chairs in the hall, looking for one with a clue stuck to it. When they found the clue, it said to look for a balloon next, and when they found the clue on the balloon, that one told them to look among the trees.

"Look!" cried Kirsty, as the three fairies flew past a big tree.

Nestled among the tree's roots was a small, sturdy chest. Its lid was open – and there, on top of a pile of chocolate coins, was the missing friendship bracelet!

Florence turned both girls back to normal, and they proudly slipped the friendship bracelets onto their wrists.

"Thank you so much, Florence," said Rachel.

Then they went to share the chocolate coins with all the children at the party!

After everyone had eaten their fill, a band started playing so people could dance.

Florence hid behind Rachel's hair, and watched the fun.

"I have to go back to Fairyland now," she said. "But I'm so glad I met you both."

"Thanks, Florence," Kirsty said. "I love my bracelet!"

"Me too," Rachel said.

Florence blew them a kiss and vanished in a puff of sparkles.

"Hooray for friends," Kirsty said, holding Rachel's hand.

"And hooray for fairies," replied Rachel. "I wonder what adventures we'll have next?"

**If you enjoyed this story,
you may want to read**

Flora the Fancy
Dress Fairy
Early Reader

Here's how the story begins...

"What a beautiful place!"
Rachel Walker cried when
she saw McKersey Castle.
Her grown-up cousin Lindsay
was having a party there
to celebrate her wedding
anniversary and Rachel was
invited, along with her best
friend, Kirsty Tate.

"It's just like a fairytale castle," Rachel said.

Kirsty grinned. She and Rachel knew all about fairies because they had met and helped the fairies many times!

Inside the castle, Lindsay showed them to their bedroom.

Rachel and Kirsty gasped with delight when they saw the huge room.

Lindsay pointed to a small door set opposite the beds. "That door leads up to the battlements," she said. "Be careful if you go up there!"

As Lindsay hurried off, Rachel opened the little door and found a staircase winding upwards.

Suddenly a chilly gust of wind blew right down into the room.

"Look, there's ice all over the stairs!" Kirsty gasped.

The girls were curious, so

they climbed the steps, holding on to the handrail. The higher they got, the colder they felt.

"My Icicle Party will be the best fun ever!" snapped an icy voice ahead of them.

The two girls crept to the top of the steps and peeped around a turret. They saw Jack Frost standing there!

Read
Flora the Fancy Dress Fairy
Early Reader
to find out
what happens next!

Discover the world of

RAINBOW magic™

- 💜 There are over 130 Rainbow Magic fairies for you to meet

- 💜 Perfect for newly confident readers

- 💜 Great for reading aloud

- 💜 Each book makes reading fun. Remember to enjoy the experience together!

- 💜 Over 27 million copies sold!

Everybody loves Daisy Meadows!

'I love your books' – Jasmine, Essex

'You are my favourite author' – Aimee, Surrey

'I am a big fan of Rainbow Magic!' – Emma, Hertfordshire

Meet the first seven Rainbow Fairies

Become a
Rainbow Magic
fairy friend and be the first to
see sneak peeks of new books.

Plus lots of special offers and exclusive
competitions to win sparkly
Rainbow Magic prizes.

Sign up today and receive our
FREE Rainbow Magic Reading Star Chart
www.rainbowmagicbooks.co.uk/newsletter